BLIND JUSTICE

I

Unveiling Truth Beyond Sight

Dr. Maxwell Shimba

Printed in the United States of America

First Printing Edition, 2023

TABLE OF CONTENTS

PREFACE

In a world that often measures justice by the clarity of one's vision, "Blind Justice" seeks to unravel the intricate tapestry of truth that lies hidden beneath the surface. This is a story that challenges our assumptions, confronts our biases, and beckons us to see beyond the visible world.

In the heart of Centerton, a city of towering skyscrapers and bustling streets, a heinous crime sends shockwaves through the community. It is here, in the shadows of doubt, that our journey begins. Detective Alex Turner, known for his unyielding pursuit of justice, and lawyer Sarah Miller, whose unwavering belief in evidence transcends her own blindness, are about to embark on a quest that will redefine their understanding of justice.

As they unravel the threads of a dark and complex case, they will encounter the echoes of corruption, the unseen scales of truth, the shadows of their own pasts, and the silent witness who holds the key to it all. Together, they will challenge the conventional notions of justice and forge an unexpected alliance in their relentless pursuit of the truth.

This is a story of resilience, of the human spirit's capacity to rise above the darkest of circumstances. It is a testament to the power of evidence, empathy, and collective action in the face of corruption and deception. "Blind Justice" reminds us that justice is not confined to the visual realm but is a universal pursuit that requires determination, understanding, and the unwavering commitment to truth.

As you embark on this journey, may you be inspired to question your own perceptions, to challenge the assumptions that guide your understanding of justice, and to contribute to a world where the pursuit of truth knows no boundaries. Welcome to "Blind Justice: Unveiling

DR. MAXWELL SHIMBA

CHAPTER 01

IN THE SHADOWS OF DOUBT

In the heart of the bustling metropolis of Centerton, tucked away in a quiet corner overshadowed by towering skyscrapers, a grim tale was about to unfold. It was a city that never slept, where neon lights pierced the night, and the pulse of life surged through its veins. But on this particular night, a sense of foreboding hung heavy in the air.

It began with a phone call that shattered the tranquil facade of Detective Alex Turner's evening. The harsh ringtone jolted him from the peaceful refuge of his modest apartment. Rubbing his eyes, he answered, his voice laced with the weariness of countless late-night calls.

"Detective Turner, we have a situation," came the terse voice on the other end.

"What's going on?" Alex asked, his instincts kicking into high gear.

"A murder, a brutal one," the voice replied, devoid of emotion.

Within minutes, Alex was on his way to the crime scene, his unyielding pursuit of justice propelling him forward. As he arrived, the chilling scene unfolded before him. A dimly lit alley, its cobblestones slick with rain, revealed the lifeless body of a young woman. Her eyes, wide open in terror, bore witness to the horrors she had endured. The community was shaken to its core.

Alex's reputation as a relentless investigator was well-known in Centerton. He had solved cases that others had deemed unsolvable, but this one promised to be different. As he approached the scene, the rain began to fall, washing away the sins of the city, leaving behind only the painful reminder of this heinous act.

The investigation led Alex down a treacherous path, one that twisted and turned through the underbelly of the city. It wasn't long before he realized that this case was more than just a murder; it was a web of deceit and corruption that threatened to ensnare anyone who dared to seek the truth.

But as Alex delved deeper into the investigation, he was forced to confront a truth of his own – the biases and assumptions that had guided him throughout his career. In the harsh light of this new case, he found himself questioning the very essence of justice. Could it truly be blind when the world was so steeped in darkness?

As he unraveled the threads of the case, he encountered suspects who defied his expectations, and allies who challenged his preconceived notions. The city he thought he knew so well revealed its hidden layers, its secrets, and its capacity for both darkness and redemption.

The rain continued to fall, each drop a testament to the tears shed for the victim and the countless others who had suffered in the shadows of doubt. Detective Alex Turner, driven by an unquenchable thirst for justice, would stop at nothing to unveil the truth, even if it meant confronting the uncomfortable realities that lay hidden beneath the surface of a city that never slept.

CHAPTER 02

THE UNSEEN SCALES

In a world where sight is often considered the ultimate arbiter of truth, Sarah Miller stood as a beacon of defiance. Blind since birth, she had dedicated her life to the pursuit of justice, armed not with her eyes but with an unwavering belief in the power of evidence and truth. Sarah's story began long before her path intersected with Detective Alex Turner's, and it was a testament to her indomitable spirit.

Sarah's journey into the realm of law was an uphill battle from the start. Born into a world that often equated justice with the ability to see, she had to overcome skepticism, discrimination, and self-doubt to realize her dream. Her parents, both lawyers themselves, had instilled in her a profound sense of justice and an unshakable determination to overcome any obstacle.

Years of tireless effort led Sarah to become a formidable lawyer, specializing in cases that challenged the very foundations of the legal system. She had a reputation for taking on cases others deemed unwinnable, driven by a belief that justice was not solely dependent on sight. It was this reputation that brought her face to face with a case that would test her resolve like never before.

The case involved the murder that had shaken Centerton to its core, the same case that had drawn Detective Alex Turner into its dark web of secrets and lies. Sarah was approached by the victim's family, who had heard of her reputation and believed that she was the only one who could bring the truth to light.

As Sarah delved into the details of the case, she encountered skepticism and resistance at every turn. Many doubted her ability to navigate the intricacies of the courtroom without the benefit of sight. But she refused to be deterred. She knew that justice wasn't about seeing; it was about understanding, about uncovering the truth hidden beneath layers of deception.

With her trusted guide dog, Luna, by her side, Sarah began to piece together the puzzle of the crime. She relied on her acute sense of hearing, her keen analytical mind, and the power of evidence. She challenged witnesses, dissected alibis, and exposed contradictions in the testimony. In doing so, she unveiled the biases that often permeated society's perception of justice, the assumption that those who couldn't see were somehow less capable of discerning the truth.

As Sarah stood before the courtroom, her voice unwavering, she made a compelling argument. She argued that justice was not limited to those who could see, that the scales were not tipped solely in favor of the sighted. She called for a reevaluation of the way society viewed and valued evidence, urging the jury to look beyond the surface and into the heart of the matter.

In that courtroom, Sarah Miller became a symbol of unwavering determination and the belief that justice could transcend the confines of the visible world. Her battle was not just for her client but for a broader understanding of justice itself. And as the trial continued, the courtroom became a battleground of ideologies, where the power of evidence and the truth faced off against the biases that had long clouded society's perception of justice.

CHAPTER 03

SHADOWS OF THE PAST

The lives of Detective Alex Turner and lawyer Sarah Miller had always been marked by shadows from their pasts, and as they embarked on this tumultuous journey to seek justice, those shadows threatened to engulf them.

For Alex, the shadows were a haunting reminder of cases left unsolved, faces of victims he couldn't save, and the relentless pursuit of justice that often came at the cost of personal relationships. He carried the weight of his own failures, the scars of a past that had shaped him into the relentless investigator he had become. The murder case that had brought him to Sarah had reopened old wounds, igniting a fire within him to ensure that justice was served, no matter the cost.

Sarah's past was a canvas of determination painted over adversity. Born blind, she had faced skepticism and prejudice at every step, forcing her to prove herself time and again. Her parents had been her guiding lights, instilling in her a profound belief in the power of truth and justice. But her journey hadn't been without its trials, and the challenges she'd overcome had only strengthened her resolve.

As Alex and Sarah's paths crossed in the pursuit of justice, they found themselves confronted with the shadows that loomed over their lives. The case they were embroiled in brought their personal demons to the surface, forcing them to reevaluate their own understanding of justice.

Alex's relentless pursuit of the case often led him to neglect the people who cared about him, pushing away those who tried to help him carry the burdens of his past. He had to confront his own obsession with justice, realizing that sometimes, the pursuit of the truth could come at the cost of one's own humanity.

Sarah, on the other hand, had always been driven by a deep sense of purpose, but the case challenged her in ways she hadn't anticipated. She was forced to grapple with the limits of her abilities, to confront the fear that her blindness might be a barrier to uncovering the truth. But she refused to let doubt define her.

Their unexpected alliance became a crucible where their pasts collided with the present, forging a bond that neither had anticipated. They challenged each other's assumptions, pushing the boundaries of conventional notions of justice. Alex's determination was complemented by Sarah's unwavering belief in evidence and the power of the unseen.

As they delved deeper into the case, they began to understand that their individual strengths could be combined to uncover the hidden truths that lay beneath the surface. The shadows that had haunted them for so long began to recede in the face of a shared purpose.

In "Blind Justice: Unveiling Truth Beyond Sight," the collaboration between Alex and Sarah was a testament to the transformative power of confronting one's past and challenging preconceived notions of justice. Together, they would navigate the murky waters of corruption and deceit, determined to bring the light of truth to even the darkest corners of their city.

CHAPTER 04

THE SILENT WITNESS

In the labyrinthine investigation that Detective Alex Turner and lawyer Sarah Miller had embarked upon, a crucial piece of the puzzle was about to be revealed: Amelia, the silent witness who held the key to unraveling the enigma of the heinous crime.

Amelia was a young woman with a haunting presence, her silence speaking volumes as she sat in a dimly lit interrogation room. Her muteness was not by choice but by trauma, a chilling reminder of the horrors she had witnessed on the night of the murder. Yet, her eyes held a story that words could not convey.

As Alex and Sarah approached her, they were met with a gaze that seemed to pierce their souls. In Amelia's eyes, they saw the reflection of the terror that had unfolded that fateful night, but they also saw a glimmer of hope, a desperate plea for justice.

The detective and the lawyer had seen countless witnesses take the stand, but Amelia was different. She was a silent observer, an embodiment of the idea that justice wasn't solely about seeing; it was about listening and understanding. With Luna, Sarah's loyal guide dog, sitting patiently at her side, Sarah reached out to Amelia in a way that transcended words. She offered her hand, a silent gesture of support and empathy.

In the days that followed, Amelia's story slowly began to unfold, painting a vivid picture of the events leading up to the murder. Her written accounts and drawings, painstakingly crafted in silence, revealed a complex web of relationships and motives. She had been a bystander, a quiet presence in the shadows, and yet, she had seen what others had missed.

Through her unique perspective, the boundaries between guilt and innocence began to blur. The initial assumptions that had driven the investigation were challenged, and the concept of blind justice took on a new and profound meaning. It became evident that justice was not just about physical sight but about the ability to truly see, to perceive the truth that lay hidden beneath the surface.

Amelia's silence had become a powerful voice, a voice that demanded that the guilty be held accountable and the innocent be exonerated. Her presence in the case was a reminder that justice was not confined to the visual realm; it was a holistic pursuit that required empathy, understanding, and a willingness to listen to the voices that society often overlooked.

As Alex and Sarah delved deeper into Amelia's testimony, they realized that her perspective was the missing piece of the puzzle. Together, they would use her silent witness to shed light on the darkest corners of the case, bringing them one step closer to unveiling the truth and delivering justice to a community haunted by doubt and fear.

CHAPTER 05

THE VEIL OF CORRUPTION

As Detective Alex Turner and lawyer Sarah Miller continued their relentless pursuit of justice, they uncovered a dark and tangled web of corruption that stretched far beyond the boundaries of the initial crime. What had started as a murder investigation had now become a battle against a shadowy network of influence and deceit.

The clues and evidence they had meticulously gathered began to point toward powerful figures within Centerton's political and economic elite. The lines between right and wrong became increasingly blurry, and the duo found themselves navigating treacherous waters where truth was a precious commodity and deception was the currency of the realm.

Their pursuit of justice led them to confront the harsh realities of a deeply flawed system. The more they dug, the more they realized that corruption had insidiously infiltrated every corner of the city's institutions, from the police department to the judiciary, and even the media. The very pillars of justice they had once relied upon were tainted, and the veil of corruption shrouded their efforts.

As they got closer to exposing the truth, their own lives were put in danger. Threats, intimidation, and attempts to discredit them became a daily occurrence. It was a test of their resolve, a crucible that challenged their commitment to uncovering the hidden truths, no matter the personal cost.

Alex and Sarah found themselves walking a tightrope between danger and determination. They had to rely on their instincts, their bond, and the trust they had built to navigate the murky waters of corruption. In their quest for justice, they became unlikely heroes, battling against powerful forces that sought to protect their secrets.

The concept of blind justice took on a new dimension as they questioned whether justice could truly be blind in a world where the scales were weighted in favor of those in power. They grappled with the realization that sometimes, the pursuit of truth could lead to a bitter reckoning with the limitations of the system they had sworn to uphold.

But Alex and Sarah were not deterred. Their shared commitment to uncovering the truth and seeking justice for the victim and the community fueled their determination. They knew that their journey was far from over, and that the battle against corruption was a fight they could not afford to lose.

As they continued to peel back the layers of the city's darkest secrets, they were left with a haunting question: Could justice truly prevail in a world where the pursuit of truth had become a perilous endeavor? The answer remained uncertain, but they were willing to risk everything to find it, no matter how veiled in corruption the path ahead might be.

CHAPTER 06

A GLIMMER OF LIGHT

As the darkness of corruption threatened to consume Detective Alex Turner and lawyer Sarah Miller in their pursuit of justice, an unexpected glimmer of light emerged. In the most unlikely of places, they found allies whose passion and dedication would prove indispensable in their battle against the shadows.

Their quest for truth had taken them to the very heart of Centerton's clandestine network, and the threats against them had never been more dire. Yet, in the darkest moments, they encountered individuals who shared their commitment to exposing the corruption that had infested the city.

The first ally to join their cause was Dr. Rachel Alvarez, a forensic expert who defied the stereotype that justice was solely a visual endeavor. Blind since birth, Rachel possessed a profound understanding of the power of evidence and the intricacies of forensic analysis. Her expertise brought a unique perspective to the investigation, challenging the notion that only sighted individuals could uncover the truth.

Next came Marcus Rodriguez, a reformed ex-convict who had once been entangled in the very corruption they sought to dismantle. Marcus had experienced the harsh realities of the criminal justice system firsthand and was determined to make amends for his past. His intimate knowledge of the criminal underworld and his unwavering commitment to justice made him an invaluable asset to the team.

Completing this eclectic group was Lily Chen, a tech-savvy hacker with a passion for uncovering hidden truths in the digital realm. Lily's expertise in navigating the dark corners of the internet and exposing secrets was a formidable weapon in their arsenal. Her ability to gather information and uncover connections that had remained hidden gave the team a significant advantage.

Together, they formed an alliance that transcended the boundaries of convention. Each member brought their unique skills and perspectives to the table, working in harmony to expose the corruption that had plagued Centerton for far too long.

Their journey was not without its challenges. They faced constant threats, both overt and covert, from those who sought to protect the corrupt system. The stakes had never been higher, and the risks they took were immense. But their shared commitment to justice and their unwavering determination fueled their resolve.

As they delved deeper into the intricate web of corruption, they uncovered shocking revelations that sent shockwaves through the city. The corruption reached higher and wider than anyone had imagined, implicating figures of authority who had long operated with impunity.

The glimmer of light that had emerged in the darkest moments of their journey grew stronger with each discovery. The team's collective action, fueled by their shared belief in justice, became a force to be reckoned with. They were no longer fighting alone; they were part of a movement, a coalition of individuals dedicated to exposing the truth and holding the perpetrators accountable.

In the heart of Centerton's shadows, where justice had once seemed elusive, a spark had ignited. The battle was far from over, but the team knew that as long as they stood together, justice remained attainable. Their unwavering determination and collective action were a testament to the resilience of the human spirit and the enduring power of the pursuit of truth.

CHAPTER 07

THE VERDICT OF HUMANITY

The trial had reached its climax, and the courtroom was charged with tension and anticipation. Detective Alex Turner and lawyer Sarah Miller, along with their dedicated team of allies, stood united in their fervent belief in the power of truth. This courtroom would become the battleground where their unwavering commitment to justice would be put to the ultimate test.

As they presented their case, Alex and Sarah knew that they were not just advocating for their client; they were challenging the very foundations of the conventional understanding of justice. Their journey had taken them through the darkest corners of Centerton, exposing corruption, unveiling hidden truths, and inspiring a movement for change.

Their argument was compelling: justice was not a fixed concept but an ever-evolving one, a reflection of society's collective conscience. It was a call for the jury to question the assumptions that had guided their understanding of justice, to see beyond the surface and into the heart of the matter.

The courtroom became a crucible of ideologies, where the power of evidence and the pursuit of truth clashed with the entrenched biases and systemic flaws within the legal system. The prosecution, representing the corrupt elite, fought desperately to maintain the status quo, to protect those who had long operated with impunity.

But Alex and Sarah, fueled by their collective determination and their belief in the transformative power of the pursuit of truth, presented a compelling case that left no room for doubt. They exposed the flaws within the system, the manipulation of evidence, and the manipulation of justice itself. Their argument was not just about winning a trial; it was about righting the wrongs that had plagued Centerton for far too long.

As the trial unfolded, the community began to rally behind the pursuit of justice. Citizens who had long been resigned to the idea that the system was unchangeable found inspiration in the courage of those who had dared to challenge it. The movement for change grew stronger with each passing day, a testament to the enduring power of the human spirit to demand accountability and transparency.

In the end, the verdict was not just a judgment of guilt or innocence; it was a verdict of humanity. It was a declaration that justice was not confined to the whims of the powerful but was a shared responsibility of society as a whole. The corrupt elites were held accountable, and the city of Centerton took a step closer to healing the wounds that had festered for so long.

The trial marked a turning point, not just in the lives of Alex and Sarah, but in the history of their city. It was a reminder that justice, though elusive, was attainable through unwavering determination, collective action, and the unyielding belief in the power of truth. As the courtroom doors closed, a new chapter began one where the pursuit of justice continued, guided by the lessons learned from the shadows of doubt, the unseen scales, the shadows of the past, the silent witness, the veil of corruption, and the glimmer of light.

BEYOND THE BLINDFOLD

As the final pages of "Blind Justice: Unveiling Truth Beyond Sight" come to a close, we are left with a profound sense of the transformative journey undertaken by its characters, Detective Alex Turner and lawyer Sarah Miller. Their struggles, triumphs, and unwavering commitment to justice have illuminated the multifaceted nature of this concept, revealing that it transcends the confines of mere sight.

The story of Alex and Sarah serves as a powerful reminder that justice is not a one-dimensional concept but a complex tapestry woven from the threads of truth, empathy, determination, and collective action. It's a reminder that the pursuit of justice requires us to challenge our own assumptions, biases, and preconceived notions.

Their journey through the shadows of doubt, the unseen scales, the shadows of the past, the silent witness, the veil of corruption, and the glimmer of light has shown us that justice is a relentless pursuit, often fraught with challenges and obstacles. It forces us to confront the harsh realities of a flawed system and to question whether justice can truly be blind in a world where power and influence often tip the scales.

But amidst the darkness, there is a glimmer of hope—a hope that justice is not an unattainable ideal but a goal worth striving for. Alex and Sarah's story inspires us to believe that, even in the face of adversity, we can make a difference. Their alliance with an unlikely group of allies demonstrates the transformative power of collective action and the strength that can be found in unity.

"Blind Justice: Unveiling Truth Beyond Sight" is not just a story; it's a call to action. It urges us to challenge our own perceptions, to seek truth beyond the surface, and to contribute to a more just and equitable world. It reminds us that justice is a shared responsibility, and it calls on each of us to play our part in the ongoing pursuit of a fair and just society.

As we close the book, we are left with a sense of hope—a hope that justice, though elusive, is attainable through unwavering determination and the belief in the power of truth. It's a hope that, like Detective Alex Turner and lawyer Sarah Miller, we can all be agents of change, working together to unveil the truth and bring justice to a world that so desperately needs it.

To be continued – Part 2

BLIND JUSTICE

II

The Resilience of Truth

Dr. Maxwell Shimba

Printed by Shimba Publishing LLC
Printed in the United States of America

First Printing Edition, 2023

TABLE OF CONTENTS

PREFACE

In the world of "Blind Justice: Unveiling Truth Beyond Sight," we return to the enduring journey of Detective Alex Turner and lawyer Sarah Miller. The echoes of their past battles linger in the background as they continue their relentless pursuit of justice in the city of Centerton. Volume 2 delves deeper into the complexities of their lives, their unwavering commitment to truth, and the challenges they face as they confront new adversaries and unforeseen obstacles.

The pursuit of justice, as Alex and Sarah have come to understand, is not a straightforward path. It winds through the intricacies of human nature, the digital labyrinth of the modern world, and the complexities of their personal lives. In Volume 2, we explore the ever-evolving landscape of their mission, where the pursuit of truth intersects with the resilience of family, the echoes of compassion, and the reappearance of old adversaries.

As they navigate this terrain, Alex and Sarah are confronted with challenges that test their limits, both professionally and personally. The lines between right and wrong blur, the shadows of corruption persist, and the pursuit of justice reveals new layers of complexity. It is a journey marked by the unwavering belief in evidence, the power of collective wisdom, and the echoes of compassion that resonate even in the darkest of times.

Volume 2 invites you to delve deeper into the world of "Blind Justice," where the pursuit of truth is an unending journey, and justice is a multifaceted concept that goes beyond mere sight. Join us as we continue to unveil the truth beyond the shadows, and as Alex and Sarah inspire us to challenge our own perceptions and contribute to a more just and equitable world.

DR. MAXWELL SHIMBA

ECHOES OF REDEMPTION

The echoes of their previous triumph still resonated in the minds of Detective Alex Turner and lawyer Sarah Miller as they embarked on a new chapter of their relentless pursuit of justice. The corrupt network they had exposed had been dismantled, and the city of Centerton had breathed a collective sigh of relief. But for Alex and Sarah, there was no rest, no final victory. The pursuit of truth was an unending journey, and they understood that it was their duty to continue.

The challenges that lay ahead were both familiar and unknown. The city's streets, once shrouded in the darkness of corruption, now seemed to beckon with new opportunities. As they faced a fresh set of cases, each unique in its complexities and nuances, they were reminded that justice was a multifaceted concept, and every story held its own echoes of redemption.

Their partnership had evolved, a bond forged in the crucible of their previous battles. Alex's relentless determination had found a counterpart in Sarah's unwavering belief in evidence, forming a dynamic duo committed to seeking the truth. Their lives had been forever altered by their battle against corruption, and they carried the weight of that responsibility with them.

In this new landscape of challenges and opportunities, they encountered adversaries who were no less determined than those they had faced before. The pursuit of justice was not without its risks, and the shadows of corruption still lingered, threatening to resurface at any moment. But Alex and Sarah had tasted victory, and they were fueled by the echoes of redemption that had reverberated through the city.

As they delved into their new cases, they found themselves navigating uncharted territory, challenging the limits of their expertise and understanding. The pursuit of truth was a journey of constant growth and adaptation, a reminder that they could never truly master the ever-evolving concept of justice.

The echoes of redemption served as a beacon of hope, a reminder that their battles were not in vain. With every case they solved and every injustice they confronted, they breathed life into the idea that justice was attainable, even in a world where corruption and deceit often reigned.

As Detective Alex Turner and lawyer Sarah Miller faced the challenges that lay ahead, they understood that the pursuit of truth was a journey without end. It was a journey that tested their resilience and resolve, a journey that required them to confront their own limitations and biases. But it was also a journey that held the promise of redemption, not just for themselves, but for a city yearning for justice and the echoes of a better tomorrow.

CHAPTER 02

WHISPERS OF DECEIT

Centerton, a city known for its gleaming skyscrapers and political intrigue, was once again thrust into the spotlight by a high-profile case that sent ripples through its corridors of power. The city's elite, determined to preserve their status and protect their well-guarded secrets, had drawn the curtains of deceit around a case that threatened to shake their foundations.

It was in this climate of political intrigue and corporate greed that Detective Alex Turner and lawyer Sarah Miller found themselves immersed. The echoes of their previous triumph had barely faded, yet they were now drawn into a web of deception that threatened to overshadow their past successes. The case was a labyrinth of motives, each more convoluted than the last, and the boundaries between truth and deception became increasingly blurred.

As they delved into the intricate case, Alex and Sarah encountered a cast of characters, each with their own agenda and secrets to protect. The city's elite, who had once wielded their influence with impunity, were now on edge, determined to maintain their hold on power. They were adversaries unlike any Alex and Sarah had faced before, formidable opponents who were willing to go to great lengths to preserve their secrets.

But amidst the whispers of deceit, Alex and Sarah found new allies. They were individuals who had been touched by the corruption that had plagued Centerton, and they were determined to see justice served. The echoes of their shared commitment to truth and justice resounded through the city, forming a chorus of voices that could not be ignored.

The case became a battleground of ideologies, where the power of evidence and the pursuit of truth clashed with the entrenched interests of the city's elite. Alex and Sarah were forced to rely on their collective wisdom, their bond, and the resilience they had developed through their previous battles. It was a test of their determination and their ability to navigate the treacherous waters of deception.

As they pursued the truth amidst the whispers of deceit, they understood that the pursuit of justice was not a solitary endeavor. It required the support of those who shared their commitment, those who refused to be silenced by the powerful and the corrupt. The boundaries of truth and deception would continue to blur, but Alex and Sarah were determined to see the case through, guided by their collective wisdom and their newfound resilience.

In the heart of Centerton, where whispers of deceit threatened to drown out the truth, Detective Alex Turner and lawyer Sarah Miller stood resolute. The echoes of their determination reverberated through the city, a reminder that justice was not a privilege reserved for the powerful but a right that belonged to all.

CHAPTER 03

UNSEEN ALLIANCES

In the intricate dance between justice and redemption, Detective Alex Turner and lawyer Sarah Miller found themselves stepping into uncharted territory. Their pursuit of truth had led them to the most unexpected of places—forging alliances with individuals who had once been on the wrong side of the law.

The city of Centerton, known for its complexities and contradictions, had a way of bringing unlikely allies together. As Alex and Sarah worked alongside reformed criminals and individuals seeking a path to redemption, they discovered that the journey to justice was not always straightforward. It was a path marked by twists and turns, where the concept of second chances took center stage.

The first of their unexpected allies was Marcus Rodriguez, a reformed ex-convict who had once walked in the shadows of the very corruption they sought to dismantle. Marcus had experienced the harsh realities of the criminal justice system firsthand and was determined to make amends for his past. His intimate knowledge of the city's criminal underworld and his unwavering commitment to justice made him an invaluable asset to the team.

Then there was Lena Callahan, a former hacker and cyber-criminal who had turned her skills toward exposing corruption. Her journey from the dark corners of the digital realm to the pursuit of truth had been a transformation driven by a desire for redemption. Her expertise in navigating the digital labyrinth and uncovering hidden secrets gave the team a significant advantage.

As Alex and Sarah worked alongside these individuals, they grappled with the complexities of their new partnerships. They understood that the pursuit of justice was not a simple dichotomy of right and wrong but a nuanced exploration of the human condition. The resilience of the human spirit was on full display, as their allies sought to redeem themselves and contribute to a cause larger than themselves.

The concept of second chances became a guiding principle in their pursuit of justice. It was a reminder that individuals could evolve, that the mistakes of the past did not define their future. Together, they embarked on a journey that challenged their preconceived notions and pushed the boundaries of conventional wisdom.

Unseen alliances formed in the heart of Centerton, where the lines between ally and adversary blurred. The path to justice, once marked by clear distinctions, now meandered through the complexities of human nature, forgiveness, and redemption. It was a journey that would test the resilience of their alliances and the depth of their commitment to the pursuit of truth.

As Detective Alex Turner and lawyer Sarah Miller navigated the complexities of their newfound partnerships, they realized that justice was not just about uncovering wrongdoing; it was also about giving individuals the chance to rewrite their own stories, to find redemption in the pursuit of a better world.

CHAPTER 04

ECHOES OF INJUSTICE

In the heart of Centerton, where the ghosts of the past lingered in the shadows, a cold case from decades ago resurfaced like an unwelcome specter. The city, still scarred by the echoes of its own history, could no longer ignore the haunting injustices that had been buried beneath layers of time and deception.

As Detective Alex Turner and lawyer Sarah Miller delved into this long-forgotten case, they were faced with the ghosts of a bygone era—voices silenced, stories untold, and justice denied. The unresolved mysteries that had haunted the city for years revealed the enduring impact of corruption and the toll it had taken on the lives of those left in its wake.

The victims of this cold case, long relegated to the shadows of Centerton's history, could no longer be ignored. Their voices whispered through the faded photographs and forgotten evidence, calling out for justice and vindication. Alex and Sarah, driven by a shared commitment to uncover the truth, found themselves reopening old wounds in their pursuit of closure.

The echoes of injustice served as a somber reminder that corruption had far-reaching consequences, affecting not only those directly involved but also the entire community. The unresolved past cast a long shadow over the present, and its impact could no longer be denied.

As they dug deeper into the cold case, Alex and Sarah navigated a landscape of secrets and half-truths, where the boundaries between right and wrong had been distorted by time and deceit. They were confronted with individuals who had much to lose if the truth were to come to light, and the stakes were higher than ever.

But the pursuit of justice had always been a calling for Alex and Sarah, and they were determined to shine a light into the darkest corners of Centerton's history. The echoes of injustice would no longer be silenced, and the truth that had long been buried would be unearthed.

In their relentless quest for closure, Detective Alex Turner and lawyer Sarah Miller understood that justice was not bound by the constraints of time. The echoes of injustice, once awakened, could not be ignored. They were committed to bringing the past to light, not only for the victims and their families but also for a city that needed to confront its own history and heal from its enduring wounds.

CHAPTER 05

THREADS OF BETRAYAL

The underbelly of Centerton, a city built on both power and deception, began to unravel as Detective Alex Turner and lawyer Sarah Miller delved deeper into their relentless pursuit of justice. The darkest secrets that had festered for years were now exposed to the unforgiving light of truth, revealing a tapestry of betrayal that threatened to tear apart the very fabric of society.

The threads of betrayal, intricately woven through years of deception, were now laid bare. Those who had operated in the shadows, manipulating the city's institutions for their own gain, faced the harsh reckoning of their actions. Alex and Sarah, driven by their unyielding determination to expose the truth, found themselves confronting adversaries who were willing to go to great lengths to protect their interests.

In this treacherous landscape, danger lurked around every corner, and the risks they took were immense. The city's corrupt elite, desperate to maintain their grip on power, stopped at nothing to shield their secrets from the light of justice. The boundaries between right and wrong became increasingly blurred as they grappled with adversaries who knew no limits.

Yet, in the face of danger, Alex and Sarah sought solace in the bonds they had forged. Their partnership, solidified through their shared battles and unwavering belief in the pursuit of truth, was an anchor in the storm. They understood that the pursuit of justice was not without sacrifices, and they were willing to face the dangers head-on, guided by their collective wisdom and resilience.

The threads of betrayal, once tightly woven, began to unravel, leaving a trail of exposed corruption and deception in their wake. The city's institutions, long manipulated by those in power, faced a reckoning that had been a long time coming.

As Detective Alex Turner and lawyer Sarah Miller navigated the treacherous waters of betrayal, they knew that the path to justice was fraught with challenges. But they also knew that their commitment to exposing the truth and upholding the principles of justice was unwavering. In a city where betrayal had been the norm for too long, they were determined to prove that the truth would prevail, no matter the cost.

CHAPTER 06

RESILIENCE IN THE SHADOWS

In the wake of their victories against the corrupt elite, Detective Alex Turner and lawyer Sarah Miller had hoped to see the shadows of corruption recede from Centerton. But as the city began to heal, a new breed of criminals emerged, adapting to the changing landscape of justice with a sophistication that left even Alex and Sarah astounded.

These adversaries operated in the shadows, leaving no trace of their crimes for traditional investigative methods to uncover. They were masters of deception, wielding technology and tactics that seemed one step ahead at every turn. The resilience of truth faced its greatest challenge yet as Alex and Sarah grappled with these elusive foes.

The city's underbelly, once dominated by overt corruption, now housed a hidden world of criminal innovation. It was a world where digital footprints vanished into the ether, where evidence was meticulously erased, and where the boundaries between legality and criminality became increasingly blurred.

Alex and Sarah were confronted with a level of sophistication that tested the limits of their resilience and determination. The pursuit of truth had always been a battle, but this new adversary operated beyond the conventional rules of engagement. They were dealing with adversaries who had adapted to the changing times, embracing the shadows of anonymity and staying one step ahead of justice.

Yet, in the face of this formidable challenge, Alex and Sarah refused to waver. Their partnership had weathered many storms, and their shared commitment to justice burned brighter than ever. They knew that the pursuit of truth demanded resilience, adaptability, and an unwavering belief in the power of evidence.

As they navigated the shadows of this new criminal landscape, they understood that the path to justice was not always straightforward. It required them to evolve, to adapt their investigative methods, and to embrace new technologies. The resilience of truth would be tested like never before, but Alex and Sarah were determined to uncover the hidden secrets and bring those who operated in the shadows to justice.

In the heart of Centerton, where shadows concealed secrets and adversaries lurked in the darkness, Detective Alex Turner and lawyer Sarah Miller faced their most formidable challenge yet. The battle for justice had evolved, but their commitment to unveiling the truth remained unwavering. They knew that, in the end, the light of truth would pierce even the darkest of shadows.

CHAPTER 07

THE UNBREAKABLE CODE

In the heart of their relentless pursuit of justice, Detective Alex Turner and lawyer Sarah Miller received a cryptic message that would lead them down a labyrinthine path filled with cryptic codes and hidden meanings. The pursuit of truth, once confined to the tangible world, now ventured deep into the digital realm, pushing the boundaries of their investigative skills and testing their resilience like never before.

The cryptic message, a puzzle shrouded in obscurity, held the promise of uncovering a truth buried beneath layers of encryption and secrecy. As they delved into the intricate code, they discovered that it was a language of its own, a digital tapestry of ones and zeros that concealed a far-reaching conspiracy that threatened to undermine the very foundations of justice.

With every line of code they deciphered, the scale of the conspiracy became more apparent. It reached into the heart of Centerton, infecting the very systems that were meant to uphold the law. The adversaries they faced were not just individuals but a shadowy organization that operated with precision and cunning.

Alex and Sarah found themselves navigating a world where every click of a keyboard and every line of code brought them closer to the truth. The digital realm was both a sanctuary and a battleground, where evidence and secrets were hidden behind layers of encryption, firewalls, and virtual disguises.

Their pursuit pushed them to the limits of their expertise, requiring them to adapt to a new landscape where traditional investigative methods were powerless. It was a world where the unbreakable code was their greatest adversary, but also their only path to the truth.

As they unraveled the secrets hidden within the code, they realized that the conspiracy extended far beyond the confines of the digital realm. It was a web of corruption that reached into the highest echelons of power, threatening to erode the very foundations of justice and the rule of law.

In the heart of Centerton, where the lines between the real and the virtual world blurred, Detective Alex Turner and lawyer Sarah Miller faced a challenge that tested their resilience, their investigative skills, and their unwavering belief in the power of evidence. The unbreakable code was a formidable foe, but they were determined to crack it open and expose the truth, no matter how deeply it had been buried.

CHAPTER 08

ECHOES OF COMPASSION

Amidst the tumultuous journey of relentless pursuit and cryptic codes, Detective Alex Turner and lawyer Sarah Miller discovered that their path to justice held unexpected intersections with the lives of those who had been forgotten by society. These individuals, whose voices had long been silenced in the cacophony of Centerton's chaos, emerged as poignant reminders that justice was not solely about uncovering wrongdoing but also about giving a voice to the marginalized and the forgotten.

Their encounters with these often-overlooked members of society resonated with the echoes of compassion. Alex and Sarah, both driven by an unyielding belief in the power of evidence and the pursuit of truth, understood that their mission was more than just exposing corruption and unraveling mysteries. It was a mission to right the wrongs, to seek justice for those who had been wronged, and to bring hope to those who had been left behind.

In the shadows of a city known for its corruption, they found individuals who had been unfairly condemned by a flawed system, their stories buried beneath layers of indifference and prejudice. As Alex and Sarah listened to their accounts, they realized that the pursuit of justice demanded empathy, understanding, and a commitment to uplift those who had been marginalized.

One such individual was Miguel Ramirez, a man who had spent decades behind bars for a crime he did not commit. His life had been stolen from him by a system that had failed to protect the innocent. Alex and Sarah's encounter with Miguel's story ignited a fire within them, compelling them to delve into the past, uncovering the truth, and seeking his exoneration.

Their pursuit of justice for Miguel was a testament to their unwavering commitment to righting the wrongs of a system that had failed the innocent. It was a reminder that compassion was an integral part of the pursuit of truth and that the echoes of compassion could resonate even in the darkest corners of a corrupt city.

As they embarked on their mission to bring hope and justice to those who had been left behind, Alex and Sarah understood that their journey was not just about exposing corruption—it was about giving voice to the silenced, offering solace to the oppressed, and ensuring that the echoes of compassion prevailed in a world where injustice often held sway.

In the heart of Centerton, where the pursuit of truth had forged their path, Detective Alex Turner and lawyer Sarah Miller found a renewed purpose—to be champions not only for justice but also for compassion, for those whose voices had been forgotten but whose stories would now echo through the corridors of power and change the course of their city's history.

CHAPTER 09

THE RESILIENCE OF FAMILY

As the relentless pursuit of justice consumed their lives, Detective Alex Turner and lawyer Sarah Miller found themselves at a crossroads where their personal lives came into sharp focus. The complexities of their own families, often overshadowed by the demands of their careers, began to weigh heavily on their hearts.

For Alex and Sarah, the pursuit of justice had been a calling, a mission that had often come at the cost of personal relationships. Their families had borne witness to the sacrifices they made, the late nights, and the dangers they faced. It was a path that had tested the resilience of their family bonds, and it was a challenge they could no longer ignore.

In the midst of their relentless pursuit of truth and their encounters with corruption and deception, they found themselves seeking reconciliation and understanding within their own families. The echoes of compassion that had guided their mission extended to their loved ones as well.

Alex grappled with the strained relationship with his father, a retired detective himself, who had always seen justice as a black-and-white concept. Their differing views on the complexities of the cases Alex handled had created a rift that needed healing. It was a journey of understanding, forgiveness, and the realization that justice, as they had come to understand it, was not always as straightforward as it seemed.

Sarah, on the other hand, faced the challenge of balancing her commitment to justice with her role as a mother. The demands of her career had often left her torn between the pursuit of truth and the needs of her family. She sought to find a way to reconcile these two important aspects of her life, understanding that the resilience of family bonds was as crucial as the pursuit of justice.

The personal challenges they faced became a central theme in their lives, as they navigated the delicate balance between their professional and personal responsibilities. It was a reminder that justice was not an isolated endeavor but one that affected every facet of their lives.

Through their struggles and their pursuit of reconciliation and understanding within their families, Alex and Sarah discovered the resilience of family bonds. They realized that the pursuit of justice could not be divorced from the relationships that anchored them, and that understanding, compassion, and forgiveness were as important in their personal lives as they were in their quest for truth.

In the heart of Centerton, where the pursuit of justice had transformed their lives, Detective Alex Turner and lawyer Sarah Miller found themselves on a new journey—one that would test the resilience of their family bonds and remind them that justice, in all its complexities, was intimately tied to the relationships that mattered most.

CHAPTER 10

ECHOES OF THE PAST

In the ever-evolving landscape of their relentless pursuit of justice, Detective Alex Turner and lawyer Sarah Miller were confronted with a chilling reappearance—a familiar face from their past battles, an old adversary seeking revenge for perceived injustices. The echoes of their earlier struggles, once thought to be receding into history, had returned to haunt them, reminding them that the pursuit of truth was an ongoing battle, one that required unwavering resilience.

The reappearance of this adversary reopened wounds that had long been scarred over. It forced Alex and Sarah to confront the ghosts of their past, to revisit the battles they had fought and the sacrifices they had made. It was a stark reminder that justice, though a noble cause, was not without its consequences and adversaries who bore grudges.

The echoes of their earlier struggles, the sleepless nights, and the moments of doubt served as a haunting backdrop to the challenges they faced in the present. It was a test of their resilience, a reminder that the pursuit of justice demanded more than just determination—it required the strength to face their past and the courage to confront the adversities of the present.

As they grappled with the reappearance of their old adversary, Alex and Sarah understood that the pursuit of truth was a never-ending journey. It was a path marked by triumphs and setbacks, victories and defeats, and the unending commitment to justice.

In the heart of Centerton, where the echoes of the past intertwined with the challenges of the present, Detective Alex Turner and lawyer Sarah Miller stood firm. The battles they had fought and the adversaries they had faced had shaped them into the champions of justice they had become. The echoes of the past served as a stark reminder of the resilience required to face the challenges of the present and to continue their unyielding pursuit of truth.

UNVEILING TRUTH BEYOND SIGHT

In the aftermath of relentless pursuits, cryptic codes, and echoes of the past, the journey of "Blind Justice: Unveiling Truth Beyond Sight" concludes with a profound reflection. Volume 2 weaves a tapestry of resilience, compassion, and unyielding determination as Detective Alex Turner and lawyer Sarah Miller navigate the complexities of justice in the city of Centerton.

As the echoes of their earlier struggles fade into the recesses of history, the characters find themselves transformed by the challenges they faced. The pursuit of justice, a journey that transcends the boundaries of conventional understanding, has left an indelible mark on their lives.

The threads of betrayal, the unbreakable code, and the shadows of corruption have been unraveled, exposing the intricate web of deceit that once ensnared Centerton. The pursuit of truth, though fraught with challenges, has revealed that justice, though blind, is a guiding light that pierces through the darkest of shadows.

In the final moments of Volume 2, our characters stand at the precipice of a new beginning. The revelations, sacrifices, and triumphs have forged a path toward a more just and equitable future. The resilience of family, the echoes of compassion, and the unyielding commitment to truth have become guiding principles that extend beyond the confines of the pages.

"Blind Justice: Unveiling Truth Beyond Sight" concludes not with an ending, but with a call to action. The epilogue invites readers to carry the lessons learned into their own lives, challenging perceptions, seeking truth, and fostering compassion in a world that often conceals its injustices.

As the echoes of the characters' journeys linger, the epilogue resonates with hope—a hope that the pursuit of justice, though arduous, is a transformative force capable of bringing about change. The journey continues, and the call to unveil truth beyond sight echoes beyond the pages of this tale, urging us all to be champions of justice in our own stories.

To be continued Part 3